Jackie and t

Molly's brother looked from Babs to me and back again to Babs, frowning slightly while we watched him in suspense. At last he seemed to have come to some decision.

'You came by horse-box, didn't you?' he said, 'so I suppose you could go back by the same means. Where is it? Is it still at the bottom of the lane or is it coming back this way later?'

I felt quite defeated. This was the end of our hopes of spending the summer helping at the pony trekking centre. I could feel tears stinging my eyes, and turned away, ashamed in case I really did weep.

'I almost wish the horse-box was coming back,' Babs was saying, rather angry. 'But he won't be. The driver was in a hurry to get home. He must be twenty or thirty miles away by now.'

'Well, now you're here,' John said, 'I suppose we'd better try to make the best of you, for a few days, anyway. But understand this . . .' He sounded stern again. 'You've got to do as you're told – ' He stared at Babs – 'especially you! Or back you go where you came from – double quick!'

Jackie and the Pony Trekkers

Judith M Berrisford

KNIGHT BOOKS

Hodder and Stoughton

First published in Great Britain in 1963 by Brockhampton Press Ltd

Knight Books Edition 1992

Printed and bound in Great Britain for Hodder and Stoughton Children's Books, a division of Hodder and Stoughton Ltd, Mill Road, Dunton Green, Sevenoaks, Kent TN13 2YA (Editorial Office: 47 Bedford Square, London WC1B 3DP) by Cox & Wyman Ltd, Reading. Typeset by Hewer Text Composition Services, Edinburgh.

British Library C.I.P.
A Catalogue record for this book is available from the British Library.
I. Title

ISBN 0 340 57050 4

For my young friend

HELEN MARGARET ASTIN

Contents

CHAPTER ONE

SOON IN DISGRACE

'Here we are!' My cousin Babs excitedly
looked across at me as we trotted our ponies
along the lakeside road. 'I *am* thrilled, Jackie.'

'Me, too, Babs.'

Yes, Babs and I felt on top of the world.
We thought that we were two of the luckiest
pony-mad girls in Britain. In a few moments we
should arrive at the Pinewoods Pony Trekking
Centre where we were going to spend the
whole of our summer holidays.

Even now we could hardly believe our good
fortune. It had all happened through my pen-
friend, Molly Collins. I had not yet met her,
but we had been writing to each other for
nearly a year. Molly was the same age as
Babs and me – thirteen – and, from her
letters, I felt I knew her really well. She
had an older brother, John, who had a job

as an instructor in a riding school outside Birmingham.

More important, she had a seventeen-year-old sister, Susan, who, with a cousin of theirs, had rented a big farm-house, named Pinewoods, in the Welsh mountains and started a pony trekking centre. Naturally Molly was planning to be there during the whole of her summer holidays, and even better, she had invited Babs and me to join her.

'*Do come*,' Molly had written in her last letter. '*There'll be Susan, cousin Tessa, and me, and all the ponies and pony trekkers. So we shall have a really super time.*' And at the bottom of the letter Susan had written: '*Yes, please come, but be prepared to help, mainly pony-jobs!*'

So here we were, nearly at Pinewoods, having alighted, with our ponies, from a horse-box that had taken us to the end of the lane. The lake was sparkling, and a kestrel soared in the blue sky above the bracken-covered mountain. On the other side of the lake was a fir forest, dense and green except where a mountain stream tumbled and foamed in a silvery waterfall.

My grey pony Misty held her head high, her neat ears pricked, and her black mane rippled by the breeze. She snuffed the scents of heather, peat and pine as though she knew that she had come home again to the Welsh mountains where she had been a foal. Yes, Misty was a Welsh pony, and I was pleased that she was obviously going to enjoy this summer every bit as much as we were.

Babs's skewbald, Patch, was a brown-and-white New Forest pony, and though Wales was not his native heath, we could see that he, too, liked the feeling of freedom amid the wilds.

Just then a woolly mountain sheep skittered out of the bracken in front of Misty. Full of high spirits, my pony shied.

Hampered as I was by my rucksack and Misty's bulging saddle-bags, I could not stop her as she broke into a canter.

I shortened my reins and struggled to slow her to a trot. Then, suddenly, I heard Babs shout.

'Look out, Jackie!'

To my surprise and alarm I saw a bay pony galloping wildly round the bend towards me. On the bay's back was a dark, curly-haired boy of about nine. He had dropped his reins and was clinging to the pony's mane. His feet were out of the stirrups, which were banging against the pony's sides, adding to its fright.

Round the bend, behind him, came a fair-haired young man astride a racy-looking chestnut mare. He looked well-turned out and efficient and was obviously riding to overtake the runaway. As soon as he saw Babs and me, he shouted:

'Hey, look out, there! Keep out of the way!'

Taking my pony, Misty, by surprise I was able to halt her by turning her into the hedge. The runaway bay pony thundered nearer and I saw a look of terror on the white face of the little boy.

'Help!' the boy called to Babs and me. 'Please do something!'

Babs shortened her reins determinedly and closed her heels to Patch's sides.

'Don't, Babs!' I told her. 'Leave it to the young man. He can cope!'

I put out a hand to grasp Patch's reins and so to keep Babs out of the way and leave a clear field. My warning was too late. Headstrong and impulsive as always, Babs had already turned Patch and ridden him straight at the bay pony.

'Get out of the way!' yelled the young man whose mare was about to overtake the runaway.

Then everything happened at once. Babs, turning her head to hear what the young man was shouting, collided with the bolting pony. The young man's chestnut mare banged against Patch, who jerked back on to his hocks in the road. The boy's pony went down, and Babs and the boy were both thrown off. The chestnut mare kept her feet, but the young man was jerked clear. I saw blood coming from a wound on the coronet of the chestnut's near fore where Patch's shoe had caught her.

I jumped off Misty. Babs scrambled up, and we both ran to the young boy who was still looking very scared.

Meanwhile the young man had made his handkerchief into a pad and was staunching the wound on the chestnut's coronet. He looked up at Babs.

'Didn't you hear me yell to you to keep out of the way?' he demanded, his eyes glinting angrily.

'Yes, but –' Babs began.

'It wasn't her fault,' piped the small boy. 'I shouted to this girl to help me. I didn't know you were so close behind me, Mr Collins.'

'Collins!' I echoed. I delved into my pocket for an envelope with an address on it and smiled brightly at the young man. 'Are you any relation of Molly and Susan Collins of Pinewoods?'

'I'm their brother,' grunted the young man, then suddenly looked at our bulging rucksacks, as though he had just realized something rather shattering, and added: 'Your names wouldn't happen to be Jacqueline Hope and Barbara Spencer?'

'Yes, I'm Jackie and this is Babs,' I said brightly.

The young man's expression of dismay deepened as he gazed at us.

'Good grief!' he exclaimed. 'I'd forgotten about you two. Oh gosh! As if I haven't got enough troubles with this pony trekking venture without having to wet-nurse two extra juveniles. How old are you?'

'Thirteen,' Babs said, trying to sound grown-up. 'And really, Mr Collins, I can't understand your attitude, because both your sisters invited us here for the summer holidays.'

'I know,' retorted John Collins. 'And Susan ought to have sent a telegram telling you not to come. I'd have sent it myself, but somehow I got the idea that you were both older. You see, I'm in charge here now. Pony trekking's too big a venture to be run by a bunch of girls.'

'But we thought you were in Birmingham,'

Babs said, hurt and puzzled, 'working as an instructor at a riding school.'

'So I was until a couple of days ago.' John stooped to wipe the blood from his chestnut's coronet, then suddenly looked up. 'But what's that got to do with you?'

'Er, nothing,' I said doubtfully, feeling that John's change of occupation would probably concern us very much indeed. 'We're Molly's pen-friends. That's why we're interested. She's mentioned you in her letters, and we thought it must be exciting for her to have a brother who is a riding instructor.'

John didn't say anything.

'Why don't we all ride to Pinewoods together?' Babs suggested blithely, gathering up Patch's reins. 'I'm longing to meet Molly.'

John wheeled round.

'That's just what you won't be doing.'

'Why?' I asked. 'Where is she?'

'A hundred miles away, in Birmingham.' John looked from Babs to me. 'And the only people she will be meeting for the next few weeks will be Mother and the doctor.'

'Oh dear!' exclaimed Babs. 'What's happened?'

'Happened!' John echoed. 'You ought to

have been told. Molly came out in spots the very day she was due to come to Pinewoods.'

'Gosh!' I gasped. 'Has she caught something?'

'Yes, chicken-pox.'

'I am sorry,' I said, stunned. 'Oh, poor Molly! What bad luck! She'll miss a lot of her summer holiday.'

'Yes, she'll be in quarantine for the next three weeks.' John stood upright and seemed to tower over us. 'Meanwhile what, in heaven's name, am I going to do with you two?'

'Now please listen.' Calmly I tried to reason with Molly's big brother. 'Babs and I have come a long way with Misty and Patch, and we've spent all our savings to hire a horse-box.'

'Yes,' Babs added, 'and even if you do let us stay, it isn't going to be much fun if we feel that you don't want us.'

Molly's brother looked from Babs to me and back again to Babs, frowning slightly while we watched him in suspense. At last he seemed to have come to some decision.

'You came by horse-box, didn't you?' he said, 'so I suppose you could go back by the same means.'

'What!' Babs wailed in dismay. 'Right now?'

'Well, yes,' John said, sounding slightly apologetic. 'Where is the horse-box? Still at the bottom of the lane? Or has it gone on somewhere and is it likely to come back this way later?'

I felt quite defeated. This was the end of our hopes of spending the summer helping at a pony trekking centre. I could feel tears stinging my eyes, and turned away, ashamed in case I really did weep.

'I almost wish the horse-box was coming back,' Babs was saying, rather angry. 'But it won't be. The driver was in a hurry to get home. He just dropped us, turned round and drove off. He must be twenty or thirty miles away by now.'

'Well, now you're here,' John said, 'I suppose we'd better try to make the best of you, for a few days, anyway. We'll see how you shape. But understand this . . .' He sounded stern again. 'You've got to do as you're told –' He stared at Babs – 'especially you! Or back you go where you came from – double quick!'

CHAPTER TWO

THE PONIES OF PINEWOODS

Pinewoods Pony Trekking Centre was as wonderful as Babs and I had imagined – a rambling farm-house among the pines with wonderful views of the mountains and the lake.

In a field behind the house were nineteen ponies. Some of them were game little mountain ponies, like Misty, and some were stocky, hairy-heeled cobs.

There were browns, blacks, tan-freckled greys, a piebald, a couple of duns and a chestnut, and all of them adorable.

Molly's sister, Susan, and her cousin, Tessa, made us feel very welcome. They showed us the caravan in the orchard where Babs and I were going to sleep because there wasn't room for everybody in the house.

Everything seemed super. But there seemed to be one snag – Molly's big brother, John.

How did two friendly girls, like Molly and Susan, come to have such a grumpy and bossy brother? Perhaps he might not really be like that. Perhaps he would be quite likeable when he saw we were two sensible girls who really could be useful with the ponies.

When I sat up that night in my bunk in the caravan with a scribbling-pad on my knee to write to Molly, I felt I had to write something about John. But it was a bit difficult to know what to say. I couldn't very well tell her that we thought her brother was sometimes grumpy and cross and that our first meeting with him had been nothing short of disaster.

Susan had already told us that she and Tessa had planned to run the pony trekking centre on their own. So it had been quite a surprise for them when John had arrived two days ago and more or less taken charge. Apparently he had had an argument with the owner of the riding school where he worked, and had walked out.

But why worry about John? I had this letter to write. I took a grip on my ball-point pen, and began to write:

Dear Molly,
   Don't worry about a thing. We've got here

safely, and we're helping to hold the fort until you're out of quarantine, and can be here with us all.

After tea, Babs and I helped Susan to feed the ponies and clean the tack. Everybody has been working like mad, getting ready for tomorrow – the Big Day when a coachload of pony trekkers is coming. At the moment, there are only Tim Fenton, aged nine, and his Mum.

Babs and I think it's bad luck that you have chicken-pox, just when we were going to meet at long last, and have such a grand time together. But not to worry! You'll be here long before the end of the summer holidays, and then you'll be able to catch up with all the pony-fun that you're missing.

I'll write often and tell you all the news, but Susan says you probably won't be able to write back in case any germs get in the letter! So I'll understand if I don't hear from you.

Dusk was now falling, and I could not see what I was writing. I would finish the letter next day. I snuggled down in my bunk.

Babs was already asleep. I could hear her steady breathing.

'Sweet pony dreams!' I murmured, and then thought about my own pony, Misty. She liked being here. She and Patch had galloped round and round the orchard, then rolled in the cool grass, and settled down to graze. Dear Misty! In my sleepy imagination I could feel the touch of her velvety nose and the tickle of her whiskers as she nuzzled against my cheek.

How I loved my pony!

'Here they are!' Babs exclaimed excitedly soon after three o'clock the following afternoon. 'The pony trekkers!'

We finished saddling the last two ponies, hastily combed our hair, and brushed straw from our clothes before rushing into the stable yard.

Susan and John were already there as the coach pulled up. John was smiling and friendly, while he shook hands with each of the guests when they alighted.

First came a plump young man in a tweed suit. He had spectacles with dark thick frames.

The other trekkers were younger. There were two girls in bright sweaters and whipcord slacks carrying blue duffle-bags decorated with the badges of places they had visited on other holidays. Then came a smart young woman, and a batch of students, boys and girls, and three teenage youths in tight trousers and suede jackets. They wore black, fun-fair, cowboy hats and looked jolly. One was carrying a guitar, while the other two had mouth-organs on which they blew cheerful blasts as they got off the bus to announce their arrival.

Susan and John showed the guests to their quarters – the boys and men to the big barn which had been fitted up as a ranch bunk house. It seemed quite comfortable and with lots of atmosphere.

All the guests stood round in groups, talking eagerly and awaiting the big thrill of meeting the ponies. Then Susan and John came out of the house. John had a big notice in his hand.

'I've written down one or two important points here,' he declared, 'and I'm going to tack this notice to the stable door where everyone will see it before going inside to feed or groom the ponies.'

While John tacked up the framed notice we all crowded round to take in what he had written out so painstakingly.

SPEAK TO YOUR PONY BEFORE GOING UP TO IT DO NOT MAKE SUDDEN MOVEMENTS

HANDLE YOUR PONY FIRMLY AND QUIETLY
BUT NOT ROUGHLY
LET YOUR PONY KNOW YOU ARE THE BOSS
ALWAYS PUT A HAND ON YOUR PONY'S NECK
OR QUARTERS AND SPEAK TO IT BEFORE
LIFTING OR INSPECTING ITS LEGS OR FEET
ALWAYS PUT A HAND ON YOUR PONY'S
QUARTERS BEFORE PASSING BEHIND IT
SMOKING IN OR NEAR THE STABLES IS
FORBIDDEN
THESE RULES ARE FOR YOUR PONY'S
PROTECTION AND YOUR OWN SAFETY

After reading it we assembled in the stable yard.

'Now,' said Susan, turning to the pony trekkers, 'I expect you're longing to meet your ponies, so we'll begin the introductions.' She smiled to Babs and me. 'Jackie and Babs, please will you bring Viking and Ranger out here?'

In pairs Babs and I led out the trekking ponies. They were bridled, saddled and wearing halters, and John and Susan allotted them to the various trekkers according to size and weight and the varying ability of the riders.

'Can you ride?' Susan asked the lankiest of the youths in cowboy hats who was called Ed.

'Certainly can,' Ed assured her, placing his foot in the stirrup of the brown cob Babs was holding and taking over the reins. 'There's nothing to it.'

Ed swung himself into the saddle with such energy that he overshot it and slipped to the ground on the other side. He picked himself up with a grin and said in a mid-Atlantic accent:

'I reckon these English saddles just don't give a fellow no foothold. Give me the Western type every time.'

'Perhaps most of your riding's been done in an armchair watching cowboy films on television, old chap,' John said, picking up Ed's cowboy hat from the grass and handing it back to him. 'But we'll make a Lone Star Ranger of you yet if you'll be content with a quiet pony to begin with.'

Soon all the trekkers had been paired off with suitable mounts, and John and Susan called everybody into a half-circle.

'When you're out on a trek,' John told the trekkers, 'you're bound to want to tie up your pony sometimes. So now I'll show you the Trekkers' Knot.'

He borrowed Misty to demonstrate.

'Move over, girl,' he said to my pony, and gave her a friendly slap on the rump. Then

Misty did something that she had never done before. She lashed out with her heels.

'Misty!' I gasped.

Misty's kick caught John in the stomach, winding him and knocking him over.

'Wow!' whooped Ed, waving his cowboy hat in the air. 'This is real rodeo stuff. But listen,' he added, helping John to his feet, 'are you hurt?'

Ed's two friends were only just managing not to laugh.

Pink in the face, clutching his middle and gasping for breath, John tried to straighten up.

I felt dreadful.

'Oh, John!' I exclaimed. 'I am sorry.'

John did not even look at me. He glared at Misty and then, pulling himself together, spoke to the trekkers:

'I ought to explain that this is not one of our trekking ponies and isn't likely to be. She's obviously a kicker and not fit to be with other ponies or anywhere near beginners.' He turned to me. 'Take Misty away and put her in one of the looseboxes.'

I went to Misty's head, taking her reins and soothing her. I wanted to argue with John, to tell him that Misty wasn't really a kicker.

Babs rushed to my side and put an arm over Misty's neck.

'It's not true.' She was determined to speak her mind. 'Misty's one of the sweetest-tempered ponies in the world. Jackie won her in an essay competition. She could have had a real "blood" pony or a hunter, but instead she chose Misty. She saw her pulling a firewood cart and persuaded the editor of *Horseshoes* to buy Misty as her prize pony.'

'Misty had been a show-jumper before she pulled a firewood cart,' I added. I wanted everybody to know the truth about Misty and what a wonderful pony she really was. 'But she'd had a fall and her rider had been hurt and lost her nerve and so Misty was sold and fell on hard times.'

'There you are!' said John. 'Show-jumping ponies don't come to pulling firewood carts unless they show vice.'

'Oh, you're horrid!' Babs blazed at John before I could stop her. 'You didn't want Jackie and me here and now you've taken a dislike to poor Misty. No wonder Misty kicked you. She knows how beastly you are!'

Already the trekkers were murmuring, some of them, I suppose, thinking we were impertinent or cheeky, and sympathizing with John who had stepped forward and was about to remonstrate with us some more.

'Come on, Babs,' I said to my cousin, leading Misty across the field. 'What's the use? No one will take any notice of what we say.'

CHAPTER THREE

THE CAUSE OF THE TROUBLE

'Why did I have to be so rude to John?' Babs groaned as we led Misty into the loose-box and removed her bridle. 'Now we shall be sent home for sure.'

I nodded. I felt too miserable to say anything.

We had worked so hard that morning, trying to show John how good we were with ponies. We had hoped to make him realize that we would be really useful and a great help to the pony trekking centre. Now it seemed that all our efforts had been in vain. Why, oh why, had it had to happen like this?

'Misty!' I gazed, puzzled, at my pony's gentle face. 'Whatever made you kick John?'

'And why did I have to make things worse by storming at him like that?' Babs groaned. 'It was bad enough for him to be put flat on his back and made to look a fool before the trekkers, without being rude to him in front of everybody.'

'That kick must have hurt, too,' I sighed. I turned to Misty. 'I don't know what got into you, girl. I've never known you do anything like that before.'

Just then we heard footsteps crossing the stable yard and Susan came through the doorway of the loose-box.

She, too, looked upset and seemed as though she was trying hard not to give us a piece of her mind.

'I'm ever so sorry, Susan,' I apologized. 'I can't understand why Misty behaved like that. She's never kicked anyone in her life. She's never even nipped. She's the sweetest-tempered pony.'

'So I would have thought,' said Susan. 'That's why I'm puzzled. John's puzzled, too. He's coming to have a look at Misty in a few minutes, and I want you two out of the way before he comes. I'd like you to go indoors and help Tessa. She's got a lot to do just now with high tea to prepare for all the guests.'

Crestfallen, we went to the kitchen. Did this mean that John had decided we were not to be trusted with pony-jobs?

Tessa, unaware of our disgrace, looked up happily as she sliced up cold chicken and apportioned it to the plates standing in rows on the long, serving table.

'Thank goodness for a bit of help!' Tessa smiled at us. 'You are angels,' she added. She handed Babs a tin-opener and a spoon and pointed to some tins of mixed vegetables in mayonnaise. 'Open these for me, and put a good dollop on to each plate. Jackie, would you be a pet and wash and dry these lettuces?'

We felt anything but pets and angels. We had behaved badly, and we knew it, and Tessa's sweet friendliness only made things seem worse. We were anxious, too, about Misty.

We were washing the lettuces and cress when Babs suddenly grabbed my arm and pointed through the window.

'Look!' she exclaimed. 'John's just gone into Misty's loose-box now to examine her. What do you think he'll find?'

'I don't know,' I said. 'And I'm too ashamed to ask him.'

'I'm not,' Babs declared, hurrying to the door.

'Come back,' I urged, pulling at her sleeve. 'John won't harm Misty. He knows more about ponies than we do.'

I felt nervous, just the same. Would Misty let John examine her? Or, for some reason or other, would she kick again or, worse still, bite? And would he then imagine she was a truly vicious pony and must be sent away?

Babs and I carried on with our kitchen jobs.

My heart sank when John strode into the room ten minutes later, while we were slicing up tomatoes and cucumber, and said briskly:

'Babs and Jackie. Come to the stable with me. There's something I want you to see.'

We followed my pen-friend's big brother to the loose-box.

'Look at this!' John said at last, pointing to Misty's quarters.

Babs and I moved nearer and I saw a raised lump beneath my pony's skin.

'See this gall?' John demanded.

'Oh dear!' I gasped, in dismay. 'I hadn't noticed that.'

'Why not!' he wanted to know. 'You groomed Misty today.'

'Yes, but I didn't have time to finish, so I must have missed that part.' I patted Misty's neck to comfort her. 'Poor girl! No wonder you kicked when John put his hand on your back. That gall must be sore.'

'It's a shame,' said Babs. 'But at least it proves one thing – that Misty isn't vicious.'

'Maybe.' John looked from Babs to me. 'But it proves something else, too – that you girls can't even look after your own ponies let alone anybody else's.'

I felt chastened. This ought not to have happened. I was to blame. I realized that the gall could have been caused by the looseness of the strap holding my rolled-up mac when we arrived yesterday. Perhaps the buckle of my mac belt had rubbed Misty.

'Misty can't be saddled until this has cleared up,' John pointed out. 'That means nobody will be able to ride her.'

'I know,' I nodded.

'So it amounts to this –' John's tone was exasperated. He obviously thought we were a couple of duffers. 'You two have been here less than twenty-four hours, but already you've put two ponies out of action – first my Daystar, with her cut coronet, and now your own Misty.'

'We're sorry.' My voice was small. 'Really we are.'

'If you go on at this rate we shall be a pony hospital instead of a pony trekking centre.'

'We'll be more careful,' I promised.

'If you get the chance!' said John, and without another word he turned and walked out of the stable. We felt very subdued.

When we went to the saddle-room to get a bucket and a packet of salt, we saw that John and Susan had been busy printing more helpful notices. They were fixed round the saddle-room walls and over the bins in the food store. One notice read:

ALWAYS WATER YOUR PONY BEFORE YOU FEED IT — OTHERWISE IT WILL GET INDI-GESTION.

Another one read:

PLEASE DO NOT FEED TOO MANY TITBITS OR YOU WILL SPOIL YOUR PONY'S TEMPER.

And another:

IF YOU BRING YOUR PONY IN HOT FROM A RIDE PLEASE SEE THAT HE IS RUBBED DOWN AND DRIED. PONIES EASILY TAKE CHILL.

And – best of all – fixed on the inside of the saddle-room door where all trekkers would see it when they went out, was the following:

KEEP YOUR HEAD AND YOUR HEART HIGH UP
YOUR HANDS AND YOUR HEELS WELL DOWN
YOUR KNEES HELD CLOSE TO YOUR PONY'S
SIDES AND YOUR ELBOWS CLOSE TO YOUR
OWN.

Having digested all this pony lore, Babs and
I hurried to bathe Misty's gall with a salt water
solution. We had just finished when the big bell
in the porch clanged to let everybody know that
tea was ready.

'There!' I said to Misty. 'You stay here
quietly, and, after tea, we'll put you in the
orchard with Patch.'

The tea looked delicious. There was chicken
and salad, rolls and butter; bowls of raspberries
and jugs of cream, and plates of Tessa's home-
made cakes.

The trekkers' eyes lit up. They evidently
thought that this was a good start to their
holiday.

'Great!' whooped Ed. 'They're not going
to let us starve at the Bar X Ranch.'

Everyone sat down and began to eat, while
Susan and Tessa poured out tea from big
brown teapots. Then, above the chatter, Tim's
mother was suddenly heard to say:

'There's one empty chair. Are we all here?'

34

Babs and I had already noticed who was missing, because we had been dreading our next encounter with him. The chicken and salad were in front of the empty chair – but John was absent.

'Yes, poor John is going to be hungry,' said Susan. 'He won't be getting his tea until much later.'

'Why, where is he?' asked Ed. 'Riding the range?'

'Well, yes, in a way,' said Susan. 'Two ponies are out of action, and he's going round the farms trying to get two more in time for the first pony trek tomorrow.'

Every bit of chicken that Babs and I ate seemed to stick in our throats. At this moment John would be feeling pangs of hunger and blaming us for that!

CHAPTER FOUR

TREKKING

Our first pony trek – and Misty could not come with us!

I could see that my pony was disappointed and puzzled as she watched us ride out of the yard next morning. She trotted along the fence whinnying and calling, longing to go with us. She could smell the exciting scents of the forest and mountains, and did not want to be left behind.

I felt that I was forsaking her.

'Cheer up, Jackie,' Babs said, riding beside me on Patch. 'She'll settle down to graze.'

I nodded and stroked the neck of the pony called Blackie that I was riding. I smiled back at Babs and made up my mind not to be down-hearted. The sun was shining; a red squirrel was scampering from branch to branch in the pine trees above our heads, but, best of all, John Collins was not with our party.

The trekkers had been split into two groups. The beginners had gone with John in one direction; and those who had done some riding were under the leadership of Susan.

Chatting and laughing, we followed the lane as it wound upwards between the fir trees. There was a wide verge at one side of the road, carpeted with pine needles.

'Hey,' a red-headed student named Pete called over his shoulder to his friend. 'How about a gallop? Come on, Mark!'

Susan had dropped to the rear of the posse to help the plump young man with thick-rimmed spectacles who was riding a brown pony and who thought that his stirrup leathers were uneven, so she was unable to stop the two boys.

Pete and Mark had already turned their two eager ponies on to the pine needles, and started off at a gallop. Blackie, the pony I was riding, threw up his head, and the other ponies got excited.

Suddenly a young woman on a grey pony shot past me. I had particularly noticed her as she was the only one of our group in really smart riding kit. She looked as though she were dressed up to be admired in Rotten Row. Her name was Miss Drew.

Her pony was determined to join in the gallop, and she could not stop him. With horror I saw her lose a stirrup and throw her arms round the pony's neck in an attempt to keep her balance.

The other ponies wanted to join in the gallop. A boy named Derek was holding back his mount with one hand and, with the other, gallantly trying to control the brown pony which a girl-student called Audrey was riding. Babs had gone to the aid of another girl.

Meanwhile Miss Drew's pony was cantering after the boys and their chestnuts.

'Help!' called Miss Drew, agitatedly trying to regain her seat in the saddle. 'Stop this pony, somebody!'

I legged Blackie after the runaway. He, too, was ready for a gallop, and, with thudding hooves, he sped after the grey. I urged him alongside, grabbed Miss Drew's reins and pulled the grey pony to a stop just as Miss Drew, unable to hold on any longer, slid to the ground.

She staggered to her feet and tenderly felt her nose. 'I got a bang from my pony's head,' she said, 'and my nose feels twice its size. Does it look swollen?'

'No, not at all,' I said, and just then Susan rode up, and took charge, apologizing to Miss Drew, who had already remounted.

The others caught up and we rode on.

A warm breeze was blowing and the air was full of the scent of pines and firs. We crossed a bridge and came to the lower slopes of the mountains. The ponies plodded on, ever upwards, and then we saw a lake shimmering in the sunshine.

Mark and Pete were by the water's edge skimming flat stones over the surface. They had tied their ponies to two young birch trees and, from the traces of sweat on their pony's necks and flanks, it was clear that they had not even thought to rub them down.

The boys turned and walked towards us as we approached. Meanwhile Susan dropped behind to help a boy who had lost his stirrup iron.

'You have been a long time,' said Mark. 'We've been waiting ages. What have you all been doing?'

'Trying to cope with the chaos that you two caused,' flashed Babs.

The two boys looked sheepish when I told

them what had happened, and explained the trouble they had unwittingly caused.

'Gosh, sorry,' said Pete. 'We didn't think.'

'Henceforth,' promised Mark, 'until everyone's ready to trot or canter, we'll go at the pace of the slowest.'

'Won't that be a bit dull for you?' asked Miss Drew. 'When my friend went on a pony trekking holiday last summer there were enough people and ponies for them to split up into several different grades. Then the ones who couldn't ride very well didn't hold back the others.'

'We don't mind,' Mark said gallantly. 'Do we, Pete?'

'We've all got to do our bit to make the trekking holiday go smoothly,' Pete agreed. 'After all, the Collinses are new to the game.'

'Quite,' Miss Drew said definitely. 'The place that my friend went to had trained instructors and, at the end of the fortnight, my friend was quite a good rider. My opinion is that the Collinses are far too young to be in charge of a pony trekking place.'

'Oh, no,' I protested loyally. 'They know more about ponies than a lot of older people. Please be patient, Miss Drew. I'm sure you'll find you'll have a wonderful time, and that everything will go smoothly – from now on.'

'I wonder,' Miss Drew said. 'But somehow I have my doubts.' She lowered her voice as Susan rode up. 'Time will tell. We'll see!'

Babs and I exchanged meaning glances. Miss Drew sounded dismally foreboding.

We soon regained our good spirits, however, as we rode through perfect trekking country. Foresters had been making a shaly road, and beside it was a log-cabin, and I thought: 'Canada must look a bit like this.' I remembered films I had seen, with columns of pine trees marching in ranks up the Canadian mountains. Here in Wales, the green showed dark against a Technicolor-blue sky and, now and then, breaks in the trees gave a glimpse of rocky bluffs where one could imagine grizzly bears lurking. Of course the only wild animals we saw were a couple of red squirrels chasing each other along the branches; and a dead badger who lay by the roadside, so still and peaceful as though he was asleep and perhaps really having a wonderful time in a badger heaven. So we managed to feel happy – even for the dead badger.

'Enjoying yourself, Miss Drew?' I heard

Susan ask, as a pine-laden breeze tempered the warmth of the sun.

'Well, yes,' Miss Drew had to admit. 'I am.'

CHAPTER FIVE

WHAT A PICNIC!

Babs and I loved trekking. We thought it was super to ride through the lovely scenery and fun to picnic in the open air, to paddle in the lakes and explore the forests.

Next day we rode to a woollen mill and watched the fast-flowing river turning the water wheel. We went inside and saw the wool being washed and dyed. Then we were shown the weaving shed where big looms were working, making thick, warm Welsh honeycomb quilts. After that we crowded into the little shop and the boys bought bright woollen caps and socks, while most of the girls bought scarves or knitting wool, and Babs and I bought woollen gloves for our mothers. Afterwards we rode back over the mountain. We had a super day.

We enjoyed helping in the stables, too, and

managed to do most things right so as not to make John angry again. Misty's gall was better, and so I was in a cheerful mood when I sat down after breakfast to write to Molly.

Dear Molly,

Today is my fourth day at Pinewoods, and Misty is coming trekking with me! Her gall has cleared up with the salt water treatment. I've been trekking on Blackie while Misty was out of action, but it will be super to ride my own pony again.

Life here really is wonderful. Susan and Tessa are great fun; the food is delicious, and the other trekkers are all youngish and a jolly crowd. One of the boys, Ed, has brought a guitar, and his two friends have both got mouth-organs, so we have some jolly sing-songs after supper.

More later – I'll finish this letter this evening when we get back from our trek.

Misty was excited as I put on her bridle and saddle, and led her to join the other ponies in the stable yard. Everybody was in good spirits and especially pleased because Susan announced that we were going to trek to a well-known beauty spot known as the Fairy Glen.

John and his party of beginners had left a quarter of an hour earlier for a Mystery Trek.

Susan's trekkers were just about to mount when the postman came up the lane in his van.

'Special delivery,' he announced.

Mystified, Susan took the envelope. She opened it and then looked relieved as she read the contents. She turned to us all.

'This might be good news!' she said, pleased. 'A few days ago John wrote to the Pony Trekking Association, asking for Pinewoods to be included in the list of Approved Centres. This telegram is to say that the Association's representative is actually coming today to inspect the place.'

'Good!' Babs exclaimed. 'If you're put on the list it means that you'll be in the pony trekking business for ever.'

'Yes, I know.' Susan's eyes were bright. 'And we wouldn't have to go back home and take dreary jobs in Birmingham.'

'Hurrah!' piped young Tim. 'Then me and Mummy would be able to come here every year.'

Susan looked flushed with excitement, and thoughtful, too.

'Now let me see. Someone will have to

be here to show the inspector round. What ought I to do? I can't ride after John because he didn't tell me the route of his mystery trek. So perhaps I'd better stay behind to cope.'

'Shall we all stay, too?' I suggested. 'We could do some polishing and cleaning up.'

'No,' said Susan. 'I think the inspector would want everything to be going on normally. He'd probably be more impressed if the guests were out on organized treks.' She looked at us all. 'Do you think you could manage by yourselves? You could? Well, here's the map.' She handed it to Pete. 'John marked the route of the trek in red ink. It's easy to follow.'

With calls of 'Good luck, Susan' we set off.

When we reached high ground, we paused to look at the wonderful views.

Below us a river curved amid meadows and forest. Ahead the mountains towered to the sky. Spruce covered their lower slopes and higher up, waterfalls showed as silver streaks on the mountain-sides.

Soon the way was so steep that we had to dismount and lead our ponies up the shaly track.

Suddenly I noticed that Tim's pony was limping. I called to the others and we halted by a tumbling stream. The ponies drank, while Babs and I helped Tim and his mother to remove a piece of shale that the brown pony had picked up in his hoof.

'This seems a good place for our picnic,' said Tim's mother, glancing at her watch and dismounting. 'It's nearly a quarter to one.'

There was nowhere to tie up the ponies, so we sat on the grass at the lakeside holding our reins in one hand and trying to unfasten our rucksacks with the other, while the ponies interestedly looked over our shoulders.

Tessa had packed up a scrumptious lunch. There were salmon patties and tomatoes and lettuce, buttered crackers with cheese between, big slices of home-made fruit cake and apples and bananas as well. There was plenty for all of us, but the trouble was that the ponies wanted to share it, too, and didn't even wait to be invited.

'Help!' wailed Audrey. 'My pony's just grabbed my tomato, and now it's after the cake.'

'Mine too,' said her friend who was named Christine, trying to push away her mount who was nosing her open rucksack. 'I just offered her a biscuit and now she wants the lot.'

We were all in trouble. The plump young

man with heavy-rimmed spectacles had been feeding his mousy-brown mare and now she was pushing and nudging his shoulder asking for more. Mark and Pete were too helpless with laughter to defend their food as their chestnut cobs snatched titbit after titbit and bolted them down.

Even Misty was naughty. Copying the other ponies, she was nudging my arm and pushing, reminding me that she, too, liked a snack.

'There you are, then, greedy.' I gave in and offered her an apple and at that moment Patch pushed right past Babs and snatched a piece of cake from my half-open rucksack.

'Oh, I am sorry, Jackie.' Babs's apology was spoiled by a giggle, but next moment it was her turn to look dismayed when the plump young man's mousy-brown mare moved forward to investigate a banana that somebody had dropped in the confusion. The mare stepped right in the middle of Babs's rucksack, squashing flat the rest of her lunch.

Then Mark's chestnut trod on his hand and after that the episode somehow seemed to stop being funny. Christine cried out as her pony – bad-tempered at not getting all the titbits she fancied – nipped her on the arm. Miss Drew, too, was in difficulties. So far she had been managing quite well by standing up to eat a little way from the others and letting her pony graze beside her. Now, however, the grey pony had caught the idea from the others and was bunting Miss Drew in the back and snatching crossly at the rucksack.

'Oh, what's the use!' Audrey exclaimed at last, standing up and tipping the remainder of her lunch on to the grass in front of her pony. 'There, you may as well finish it . . . you greedy animal!'

I think we all must have felt hungry as we rode on. I know I did, and what made us feel hungrier still was the sight that we came upon about a quarter of an hour later.

In the garden of a cottage a dozen or more riders were sitting down to lunch at a long trestle table. Plates of ham and salad, bread and butter and cakes and buns of all sorts were waiting to be eaten. Open bottles of lemonade – a straw standing in each – were ready to cool thirsty throats.

'Look,' said Babs, pointing to some ponies which, with their saddles removed, were grazing in the field at the side of the cottage. 'Ponies! Other trekkers! There must be another trekking centre near here.'

'They're luckier than we are,' groaned

Audrey. 'I wish we were sitting down to a meal like that.'

I wished the same, but I stifled my pangs and said consolingly: 'And so we will be when we get back to Pinewoods this evening.'

There were other groans. I'd merely reminded everyone how long it was until the next meal.

Then suddenly my hunger was forgotten in surprise, because a handsome young man, with dark curly hair and sun-tanned features, leapt from his place at the table, gave a quick whoop of delight and shouted towards us.

'Well, hello, Esmé. Fancy seeing you of all people!'

Miss Drew pulled up her pony, and smiling with pleasure, slid to the ground to talk to him. The rest of us moved on, and waited a few yards ahead, while Esmé Drew and the young man chattered as though they were the only two people in the whole wide world.

'I scent romance,' Tim's mother whispered to me. 'Come on. We'd better ride on slowly and give them a chance to be alone.'

CHAPTER SIX

BY THE WISHING-WELL

Babs and I were sometimes scornful about people who are in the 'sloppy' stage, but I must say we were quite intrigued when Miss Drew, in a flutter of excitement, caught up with us and told us all about the handsome young man.

'Isn't it a small world?' Her eyes were shining. 'I never thought I'd see Ronald Green in the wilds of Wales. He works for a computer firm, and sometimes calls at our office. He's a charming man.'

I heard a great deal more about the wonderful Ronald Green, and the highlights of life and work in Miss Drew's office. I was only half-listening because there was so much to look at all around us. We kept following the forest road as it led through plantations of young trees. Then we came to taller trees, some of which had been felled, sawn into fence-post lengths, and stacked in piles. Now and again we saw notices, reading 'Bryn-Glas Forest. Take care. Do not start fires.' Beside the notices were long-handled shovels and brooms for fire-beating, just like the ones at the fringe of the forest near Pinewoods.

Soon the forestry road led downwards to join the main road. We crossed a bridge over a river and came to a sign reading: TO THE FAIRY GLEN. We rode our ponies up a track and came to a cottage where chalked on a slate were the words: *Admission to the Glen 50p* – and even more welcome – *Chocolate and Lemonade sold here*.

We tied our ponies to the fence by their halters and inspected the stock of chocolate, soft drinks, sweets and biscuits that the cottage had to offer. Then, when everybody had quenched their thirsts and bought biscuits and chocolate to keep up their strength until tea-time, we paid our money and crossed the field to the brink of the tree-lined gorge known as the Fairy Glen.

Rocky crags towered above the river which foamed and tumbled over boulders in a series of rapids. Ferns, kept moist by the spray, grew in the crannies of the rocks and even on the trees themselves. Sunlight filtered through the leaves in golden bars, ending in rainbows where the sun lit up the spray.

'Fairyland!' Babs gasped, enraptured. 'And look – a wishing-well!'

I saw that the swirling river had worn a 'bowl' in the rocks. At the bottom of the bowl we could see coins that had been thrown by other people as they made their wishes. When it came to my turn I threw my coin, shut my eyes and wished that the inspector would make a good report about Pinewoods so that Susan, Tessa, Molly and John could make a success of their pony trekking centre and not have to go back to stuffy jobs in Birmingham.

Then I picked up a white pebble from the side of the well, and put it in the pocket of my trousers, hoping that the pebble might help to bring luck and make my wish come true.

After we had all wished, we went back to the ponies, and Mark and Pete unfolded the map, and looked for a different way home.

'We'll ride over the moor to Bwlch-Glas,' decided Pete. 'Then we can cut across this ridge . . .' He pointed to the map. 'That should bring us to the lake below Pinewoods, and we can ride home along the forestry track on the far side.'

A breeze ruffled the ponies' manes, and streamed out their tails as they cantered on the soft turf of a moorland track.

At the summit of a heather-clad hill, Mark called for a halt. Nearby was a peaty hollow, where the brackish waters of a moorland tarn reflected the blue of the sky.

We walked our ponies into the shallow water to cool their legs. Some of the ponies put down their heads to drink. A moorhen scudded in alarm into the reeds, her fluffy chicks paddling after her.

Misty stood with the water almost up to her hocks. She was loving it, and I had to keep a tight hold on her reins to prevent her going in deeper. Beside me was Babs, on Patch. Her pony was not as tall as Misty, and Babs had to raise her feet in the stirrups to prevent them getting wet.

Suddenly I heard splashes and looked round to notice that Miss Drew's grey pony was pawing at the water with his off-fore. To my horror, as I watched, I saw the pony begin to crouch. This was dreadful. I knew only too well what the grey pony intended to do next. He wanted to roll in the water, perhaps to cool his back where the saddle had made him hot.

'Look out, Miss Drew!' I yelled. 'Your pony's about to lie down. Kick him on.'

'Get his head up!' shouted Babs. 'Make him move!'

Miss Drew hardly had time to look alarmed. My warning had come too late. Before any of us could do anything, the grey pony turned sideways and slid down into the water. I jumped off Misty and ran to pull Miss Drew clear before her pony rolled.

Babs retrieved Miss Drew's riding hat as it floated away. Water dripped from Miss Drew's jacket and we were both knee-deep in the tarn as I helped her to her feet.

'Just look at me!' Miss Drew wailed, as she staggered to the shore. 'I'm drenched. This could never have happened in a properly organized pony trekking centre. It's wrong to let people like us out on our own, without proper instructors. Oh, I wish I'd gone to the same pony trekking place as Ronald Green!'

We all tried to comfort and help her, mopping down her clothes with our handkerchiefs.

'What's the good of doing that?' she exclaimed, brushing aside our help. 'I'll have to ride back to Pinewoods before I can get dry.'

Meanwhile Mark had grabbed the grey pony by the reins, and had dragged him to his feet, and brought him to the bank. Dripping, we stood in a group, still sympathizing with Miss Drew, who had had a worse ducking than us.

Babs and I tore handfuls of grass and heather and began to rub down the grey pony, while the plump young man with heavy spectacles took off his jacket and lent it to Miss Drew.

Then we all decided that, for Miss Drew's sake, we ought to ride straight back to Pine-woods.

We were briskly trotting along the ridge path when we saw a group of other riders.

'Wonders never cease!' said Babs. 'We meet the White Heather pony trekkers again. What fun!'

'Fun!' groaned Miss Drew. 'Not for me!' Her wet hair hung limply down her streaky face. 'What will Ronald Green think when he sees me?'

I felt very sorry indeed for Miss Drew, and wondered apprehensively what Ronald Green would do when he saw her looking such a wreck.

CHAPTER SEVEN

DANGER AT TORRENT FALLS

Yes, *Miss Drew really was looking a terrible fright* . . . I wrote to Molly that night.

Ronald Green seemed startled, but made a really tremendous fuss of her. However, Miss Drew was not pacified, and when we got to Pinewoods she burst into the tack room and told Susan what had happened. She said she had decided she wanted to leave Pinewoods because she felt that there weren't enough instructors to supervise the treks. She didn't want any more disasters, thank you! When Susan asked her where she intended to go, she said she was going to the White Heather Trekking Centre because they seemed to be properly organized!

My guess is that the main reason she

wants to go there is to be near her precious Mr Ronald Green!

But the dreadful part of it all is that the inspector from the Pony Trekking Association was within earshot – in the office that leads off the tack room, with the door open, making notes about his inspection!

Goodness knows what he thought, or whether it will ruin Pinewoods' chance of being put on the list of recommended centres. We shan't know for some time because the inspector said that he would make his report to the Association and that Susan and John would hear the decision in due course.

So we're all in terrible suspense. Without the Association's backing, Pinewoods really can't be expected to carry on successfully, particularly as there is such a super, terrifically-organized rival centre as the White Heather so near.

As you may imagine, your brother, John, was wild when he heard the news. He seemed to think that Babs and I ought to have been able to stop Miss Drew getting a ducking. He says that in future Babs and I have got to go on treks with him and the beginners, so that he can keep an eye on us.

Yet again, we are in disgrace.
Well, not to worry! More news later.
Love, Jackie.

Next morning, as he had said he would, John made Babs and me join the beginners' trekking party.

'We're riding to Llewellyn's Castle today,' he announced, as we all lined up to have our ponies and tack inspected. 'We'll make for the bridge above the woollen mill and then cut across the hill to the old church. Babs and Jackie, you ride in front and remember, walking and trotting only. Trekking is tiring for the ponies, so keep to a steady pace. I'll be at the back. Wait for me before turning of for crossing any roads.' He glanced at the trekkers. 'Right, everybody? Mount. Walk on . . . in single file.' His voice rose as Ed and his companions jogged out of the yard three abreast. *'Hey, I said single file!'*

I turned my head and saw Ed salute with a cheeky grin.

'Take it easy,' Ed breezed. 'This is a pleasure trek – not a cavalry route march.'

Babs rode in front with Patch, and Misty and I followed just behind her. We walked at first and then, when we came to the lake where everybody would have liked to linger, John called: 'Trot.'

After leaving the lake, our route led through pinewoods until we crossed the bridge over a gorge. Then we followed a track up a steepish hill.

Soon we passed an old church, and cut through the forest to Llewellyn's Castle, where we tied up the ponies and each paid our entrance fee to the gatekeeper. The castle was a fortified manor house which had been restored. Its mullioned windows and grey stone was mellow in the sunlight. Peacocks strutted in the courtyard and basked on the old walls.

We spent about an hour at the castle and then mounted to ride on to the famous Torrent Falls.

We were trotting along the main road when John called to us to halt.

'My pony's got a loose shoe,' he told us. 'I'll have to ride back to the village by Llewellyn's Castle, and get the blacksmith to fix it. In the meantime you others can ride on to Coed Celyn. You'll find a carpark in the woods opposite the Bluebird Café. You'll be able to picnic there while you wait for me.'

As John rode away, we sang: 'Get along little dogie' and soon covered the two miles to Coed Celyn. We stopped in the village and Ed and Babs went into a sweet-shop to buy ice-cream cornèts for all of us while we held their ponies. Then Helen and Diane, who worked in a London beauty parlour together, called at the chemist's to buy films for their cameras. At last we rode on until we came to the Bluebird Café and the carpark where John had told us to wait.

The carpark was a clearing among the pine-trees with the scent of honeysuckle wafting from a holly thicket and mingling with a res-inous smell from a pile of newly-cut logs. Mossy paths led through the woods and, from somewhere nearby, came the roar and crash of swiftly-flowing water as the river foamed and fretted below the two-hundred-foot drop of the Torrent Falls.

'This calls for a look-see,' declared Ed. 'Come on folks.'

With a film-Western flourish of the reins he clapped his legs to his pony's sides and jogged down the ferny path in the direction of the river.

We all followed. The roar of the water got louder and spray made a damp mist among the trees where Ed halted above a rocky gorge and waited for us to join him.

It was a wonderful sight. Between narrow, cliff-like banks of rock the river frothed and tumbled over huge boulders. We seemed to be looking down into a bubbling cauldron of white foam. A narrow path led down to a wooden bridge that tilted at an angle to a rocky ledge on the other side.

'I'm going down there,' declared Ed and, before any of us could stop him, he rode his pony forward.

Ed's pony moved cautiously, making sure of its foothold on the spray-wet rock. We saw its hind-quarters sway as it rounded a bend and followed the zigzag path towards the wooden bridge. Suddenly there was a shout from Ed and a frantic scrabble of hooves on rock. Babs and I dismounted and ran to the path. We looked down to see the pony, with Ed tugging desperately at its reins, slithering and plunging as it struggled to keep its balance on the wet, green slime on the rocky edge below.

'Keep still, Ed!' Babs shouted, running down the path to help. 'We're coming!'

But we were too late. By trying to keep the pony upright, Ed had thrown it completely off its balance. There was a final scrape of hooves on the treacherous slime of the rocks, a yell from Ed, and a scream from the pony as it plunged into the foaming torrent. Babs and I ran to the edge, hardly daring to look.

Ed was there, thrown clear, staggering dazedly between the boulders.

But where was the pony?

Babs gripped my arm as we realized the truth.

Somewhere, down there, out of sight amid the foam and swirl of the river, was a little brown pony!

What could any of us do to save him?

CHAPTER EIGHT

A PONY IN PERIL

Swaying, Ed staggered to the edge of the torrent, while the rest of us scrambled down the rocks. Then the pony's head appeared amid the foam. His eyes rolled with terror. He was swiftly being carried by the current towards the boulder-strewn rapids a few yards away.

Ed was about to go into the racing river to try to help the pony, but Babs pulled him back.

'Don't, Ed,' she pleaded. 'You wouldn't have a chance.'

I knew she was right. Nobody could swim in that raging water. We watched, in horror. Nothing could be done to save the pony – nothing.

The pony's foam-flecked head turned towards us as though in appeal, his nostrils flaring red from fright.

Suddenly his head seemed to jerk as though

it was pulled, and then he was held steady in the current while the water swirled past him.

'Look!' Babs pointed to a smooth, water-worn boulder. 'Brownie's reins have caught round that rock. But – oh gosh!'

She broke off and gripped my arm in suspense.

We saw the reins were slipping on the smooth surface of the boulder. Inch by inch the leather was moving. In a few moments the reins would have worked free, and Brownie would be swept against the cruel boulders of the rapids.

Just then something made me look up towards the other side of the gorge. Someone was waving and apparently shouting, although we could not hear a word above the tumult of the crashing water. I recognized Miss Drew. A group of people with ponies were on the path . . . the White Heather trekkers! They must have just arrived.

An agile, wiry man was already running down the rocky steps. As he ran, he was knotting a rope round his waist. Some of the trekkers were following him.

Within a few moments, the man plunged, fully-dressed, into the torrent. With the rope round his waist he struggled towards Brownie, while half a dozen trekkers strained on the other end of the rope and manoeuvred their way to the bridge, so that they could hold him steady in mid-river.

I held my breath. Could the man save Brownie? Was it humanly possible in such a maelstrom of angry water?

My heart leapt. Luck was with us. A swirling eddy carried the man towards the boulder. His hand rose from the water to grab at the slipping reins – too late!

I was in despair. Just as the man was about to grip the reins, they slid off the rock, and Brownie was again swirled towards the rapids at the mercy of the racing current.

Seeing what had happened, the trekkers on the bridge quickly let out more rope so that the man on the other end was also carried down-river. It was a desperate attempt. How could the man on the end of the rope gain the few yards needed to reach Brownie?

I shut my eyes. I just could not bear to look any more. Nothing could stop Brownie from being battered to death against the rocks.

I heard Babs's excited shout above the roar of the water.

'He's doing it!' she shouted into my ear.

'Oh, Jackie! I've never seen anything like it. Come on, Brownie! Come on, boy!'

I opened my eyes, and my hopes rose again. In the few seconds that my eyes had been shut, both man and pony must have been swirled by a side-eddy into a less turbulent patch of water – a backwater, partly enclosed by big rocks.

Everyone was shouting now.

'Fight for it, Brownie!' My voice was hoarse. 'You can make it! Try! Try!'

Half-choked by water, Brownie was striking out with his forelegs, threshing the water, trying to swim against the current. He was not making any headway; in fact he was being carried backwards, but slowly, inch by inch, the man on the end of the rope was getting nearer to him.

'Hurrah!' I cheered, and the others joined in as the man grabbed Brownie's bridle and slipped the rope off himself to put it round the still-threshing pony. Holding on to the rope, he gave a signal to the trekkers to pull. Manoeuvring themselves and the rope from the bridge back to the path, the trekkers pulled Brownie and his rescuer to a pebbly bank where they could scramble ashore.

Meanwhile, after having tied up our ponies, we all raced over the bridge in time to thank the man as he staggered ashore, and led Brownie on to a patch of grass. The pony could barely walk. As soon as his feet touched the grass, Brownie sank exhausted to his knees, and then rolled over on to his side gasping and choking.

'What a terrible thing to have happened!' Miss Drew moaned. 'How dreadful! And where's John Collins?'

'Not here – mercifully,' Babs sighed, looking up as she and I knelt by Brownie's head, cleaning river weed from his mouth and nostrils with our handkerchiefs. Meanwhile Brownie's rescuer, having slightly recovered from his own ordeal, was rubbing down Brownie vigorously with handfuls of grass, trying to restore his circulation.

Water trickled from the pony's mouth. He gave a snorting gasp, and shuddered because he was finding it painful to breathe.

His rescuer looked towards Babs. 'Run to the Torrent Falls Hotel,' he said, 'and telephone for Captain Evans, the vet. His number is Llanfair 28. Tell him to bring what he needs to restore a half-drowned pony. Hurry! There's not a lot of life left in this fellow. He could still die on us.'

While all this was happening I was aware of

the shocked chatter of the pony trekkers, but I didn't particularly listen until I heard Miss Drew, who, with her friend, Ronald Green, in attendance, was saying to two of our girl trekkers from Pinewoods:

'This is yet another example of the sort of accident that can happen if pony trekking isn't properly supervised. Am I glad that I changed over! Really the White Heather is marvellous – Mr Rorkins – he's the man who went in the water after the pony – is splendid – just splendid! He thinks of everything. He even carries a rope on every trek in case of emergencies.'

I looked across at Miss Drew, wishing that she would stop stirring up revolt among our trekkers. Then, trying not to listen, I kept my mind on Mr Rorkins, thanking him for what he had done, and helping him to rub down Brownie who now seemed to be breathing more easily. Meanwhile, some of the other Pinewoods trekkers were telling Ed what an idiot he was to have been showing off at the edge of the gorge.

Suddenly, I felt a touch on my arm, and Miss Drew was beside me.

'I'd like a word with you, Jackie,' she said, 'in private.'

Puzzled, I let her lead me away from the others. I felt uncomfortable.

'I've been so worried about you and your friend, Babs.' Her eyes were sincere. She meant well. That was clear. 'I'm not trying to make trouble. But I would like you to listen to what I've got to say.'

I kicked at a tuft of grass.

'Go on,' I sighed.

'Well, I may as well be quite frank,' said Miss Drew. 'I think it's quite disgraceful how John Collins treats you and Babs. He grumbles at you and gets cross when, all the time, it's obvious that you're doing your best.'

'We've made a lot of mistakes –' I said cautiously.

'And you'll make more if he makes you nervous by grumbling at you so much.' Miss Drew seemed quite heated. She felt strongly about this. So did Babs and I, for that matter! 'Now don't think I've been disloyal, Jackie, but I felt I had to tell Mr and Mrs Rorkins about it all, and they told me to find out whether you and Babs would like to move over to the White Heather, and help them.'

'We couldn't desert Susan and Tessa!' I said.

'But think, Jackie, what a wonderful time

you'd have,' Miss Drew tempted. 'Trekking in the daytime and in the evening films about ponies, dancing, sing-songs, and visits from famous horsy people. Guess who's coming at the weekend?'

'Who?'

'Pam Whyte!' Miss Drew announced in triumph.

Pam Whyte! She was my heroine. She was about the most famous show-jumper there had ever been – the owner and rider of the Olympic Bronze medallist mare – Acushla!

'She's bringing her famous horse,' Miss Drew went on, 'and she's going to give a jumping display.'

Pam Whyte and Acushla! In person! I was badly tempted. Why should Babs and I stay at Pinewoods out of loyalty when John did not want us?

'Think about it, Jackie,' Miss Drew said finally. 'Telephone Mrs Rorkins later.'

I nodded and went back to Brownie. He was still lying on the grass, but now he was weakly lifting his head as though he would soon want to try to stand.

'Hello, Brownie.' I knelt to stroke his neck. 'So you've decided life's worth living after all.'

I was trying to stifle the thoughts that Miss Drew had prompted – the prospect of wonderful times at the White Heather, with Mr Rorkins being kind and helpful, instead of shouting at us as John did; Pam Whyte talking to me and Babs – giving us her autograph, perhaps even letting us stroke Acushla!

Suddenly I remembered Molly, my pen-friend and John's and Susan's sister. I thought of the snapshots Molly had sent to me, and her friendly letters. There she was – in Birmingham, with chicken-pox, counting the days until she was able to come to Pinewoods, and meet all the ponies and us.

Just then Misty whinnied and I ran across to her.

'I've made up my mind, Misty,' I said, quietly, putting an arm across my pony's neck. 'I won't even tell Babs. Then she won't be tempted.' Misty turned her head to nuzzle my shoulder. 'Yes, Misty, we'll stay at Pinewoods for as long as John will let us.'

CHAPTER NINE

THE FATEFUL LETTER

What a lot I had to tell Molly in my next letter!

My hand felt cramped as I sat up in my bunk in the caravan, with my writing-pad on my knee. Already I had written two pages.

> *You can imagine how angry John was when he got to the Torrent Falls after having Daystar's shoe fixed. He told Ed he was a menace, that he was giving him his money back and that he was to leave Pinewoods the next day.*
>
> *Ed's friends, Ken and Charlie, said that if Ed was being kicked out, they would go, too.*
>
> *'And good riddance,' said John.*
>
> *Then when we got back to Pinewoods, Helen and Diane told Susan that Miss*

Drew was having a simply wonderful time at the White Heather, and that if she didn't mind, they would transfer themselves there, too.

So, in one swoop, we've lost five trekkers! Altogether six have now gone, counting Miss Drew. There are only thirteen left. Unlucky thirteen? We shall see!

Oh, I've forgotten to tell you the most important news of all – about Brownie!

It was like a miracle how, minute by minute, he seemed to pull round. The vet gave him an injection, and soon he was able to stand. Then John and Mr Rorkins led him to a stable at the Torrent Falls Hotel, and gave him some warm water with half a pint of beer in it! Later, he had a bran mash. John stayed with him until bed-time, and tomorrow he is going to get a horse-box to bring him back to Pinewoods. He'll need complete rest and quiet for several days, the vet said.

Dear Brownie! He's such a lovable pony – a real pet, with furry ears and a mealy nose.

He's everybody's friend, and when he's in the field he stands at the railings waiting to 'talk' to everybody who comes by.

That's all the news. More in a day or two.

Love, Jackie.

Babs and I were very busy for the next few days. Most of John's time, when he wasn't trekking, was taken up with looking after Brownie. So we had to fit in his share of the stable routine along with our own.

Some of the trekkers liked to help, and it was rather jolly, feeding and grooming the ponies together. Tim's Mum had got a radio, and, in the evenings, she put it on the tack-room bench while we saddle-soaped and metal-polished to the music.

Babs and I helped Tessa, too, because she had quite a lot to do getting meals for all of us. As we dried dishes and prepared vegetables we had lots of heart-to-heart chats, and so learnt just what Pinewoods and the carefree open-air life meant to her and Susan. They'd been planning and saving up for years, and then an aunt of Tessa's had left her a few thousand pounds, so they had rented Pinewoods from the Forestry Commission, and spent the legacy, and all their savings, on ponies and equipment.

Tessa never grumbled at us, not even when

Babs absent-mindedly put salt instead of sugar into the bedtime cocoa, and it all had to be thrown away! We did not mind how hard we worked for Tessa, and sometimes we did not go out trekking so that we could help.

One afternoon, Tessa told us that the groceries had not been delivered and that she had nothing – absolutely nothing – for the trekkers' high tea.

'They'll be famished when they come in,' she told us. 'And I can't get the grocer on the telephone. The line must be out of order, because it's not closing day.'

'Don't worry, Tessa,' Babs said. 'Give us a list of what you want, and we'll take our rucksacks, and ride down the valley to Capel Bach.'

We were just going through the doorway when we almost collided with the postman.

'The London mail got held up at Crewe today,' he told us. 'So I'm late on my rounds.'

As he held out a letter I could not help noticing the Pony Trekking Association's badge on the corner of the envelope.

Was this the letter which could seal the fate of Pinewoods?

'Do open it quickly,' I urged Tessa, 'and tell us whether Pinewoods has passed the inspection and is going to be recommended.'

I saw Tessa's fingers tremble as she ripped open the envelope and took out the letter. Babs and I watched in suspense, and then, next moment, we saw her give a trying-to-be-brave smile, and we knew that the news was bad.

Turning away, she handed the letter to us.

The typewritten words became blurred in front of my eyes as I read:

After due consideration of our Inspector's report made following his visit to your establishment on 22nd July, we regret to have to inform you that the committee has decided we cannot, at this time, put you on our list of recommended establishments.

Babs was the first to speak. 'Who cares?' she demanded indignantly. 'Stuffy old egg-heads! We'll manage without their recommendation.'

Tessa turned, looking the picture of defeat.

'You don't know the worst of it.' Her voice was flat. 'All the pony magazines are refusing to print advertisements from any trekking centres that are not recommended by the Association. According to last week's *Stable News*, there have been complaints about badly-run trekking places.'

'That's a blow,' I groaned. 'But can't Pinewoods manage without advertising?'

Tessa shook her head. 'We're booked up only until the end of August. If we don't get any trekkers in September and October, we shan't have enough money for the ponies' winter keep.' She broke off then and looked at us. 'I oughtn't to be worrying you two about this. Please don't let Susan and John know that I've told you.' She glanced at the clock. 'Goodness! The trekkers will be back at half-past five. Hurry and go for the groceries now.'

'We'll take the short cut,' said Babs, and we ran out to saddle our ponies.

Misty and Patch were in high spirits, but Babs and I felt subdued by the bad news. If we hadn't been so down-hearted we would have enjoyed the canter over the soft pine needles that carpeted the lakeside path. But we could think only about Tessa, Susan, and Molly and how much Pinewoods meant to them and how remote was their chance of being able to make the place pay. Six trekkers had already left during the first fortnight. I shuddered as I thought of the disasters that had led to their departure. Running a pony trekking centre was much more hazardous than one would have thought – even when people with real pony knowledge, like John and Susan, were in charge.

I suppose it was because my wits were wandering that I did not notice an overhanging branch until it knocked me from the saddle.

I landed with a thud and then for a few moments I just lay where I had fallen, without trying to get up.

'Jackie! Are you all right?' Babs was asking urgently.

'I th-think so.' Gingerly I sat up and felt myself all over. 'No bones broken.' I took Babs's hand as she held it out to help me to my feet. Then I breathed deeply. 'I'm better now. I must have knocked my head and sent myself silly for a moment when I fell. Come on. We mustn't lose time. The rest of the trekkers will move over to the White Heather if they're kept waiting for their tea.' I looked for my pony. 'Where's Misty?'

'I expect she's waiting round the bend.' Babs looped Patch's reins over her arm and walked beside me. 'She was probably scared when you fell off. She wouldn't go far. She'll be grazing at the side of the path, I dare say.'

When we rounded the bend there was still no sign of Misty. She must have been more scared than Babs thought. Perhaps she had galloped some distance.

'Misty,' I called. 'Where are you?'

I wished so much that I might hear her familiar whinny or the thud of pony hooves. But everywhere was silent. 'Misty!' I called frantically. 'Misty!'

CHAPTER TEN

PONY FARM

'Misty!' I kept shouting. 'Misty!'

I tried whistling for my pony in the way that I often did when I took titbits out to her in the field at home.

There was still no sign of Misty. Dread was rising in my heart as I ran along the forest path with Babs and Patch pounding beside me. What a place to lose a pony! Miles of forest and mountain were all round us, with a network of paths, and, as hazards, precipices, screes, the open shafts of disused lead-mines and patches of peat bog.

Then, from not very far away, we heard ponies whinnying, and our hopes rose again. Panting, we hurried round another bend and were now out of the forest. We gaped at the wonderful sight ahead of us. We had come upon a valley of ponies. There were green fields, neatly fenced and all full of ponies. There were browns and strawberries, greys and blacks, blue roans, duns and chestnuts. They seemed to be everywhere, scores of them. But where was Misty? She must be somewhere near because the other ponies had been whinnying to her. I scanned the sandy path winding between the fields and past a low, white farm-house, but I could not see my pony.

Suddenly Babs caught my arm: 'Look, Jackie!' She pointed to the second field where ten or twelve ponies were trotting and wheeling.

Sure enough, there was Misty.

With her bridle flapping and stirrups banging, my grey pony was excitedly cantering among the Welsh ponies.

'It must be a Pony Farm,' I gasped, 'and Misty must have jumped the fence to join the others.' I put a hand on the top rail of the fence and a foot on the bottom to climb over. 'Misty! Come here, girl!'

Meanwhile Babs was tying Patch's reins to the fence. Patch was neighing, calling to the other ponies, who turned and came cantering down the field towards him.

'Misty! Come here,' I called, but my pony did not listen. She was too excited at being among all the other ponies to care, or even to notice, that I was calling her.

Babs clambered into the field to join me and we ran among the cantering ponies, trying to catch Misty. Up and down the field we went, and round and round, in the midst of flying manes and tails and thundering hooves. We were in the middle of a stampede, and Babs and I were breathless and half-doubled up with a stitch long before we got near Misty.

I leaned over and grabbed her reins. Then Babs caught a stirrup leather and we managed to slow her down. That wasn't the end of our troubles. The other ponies followed us, crowding round and jostling as we led Misty towards the gate.

Babs held the gate open while Misty and I sidled through. Then one of the crowding ponies trod on Babs's foot, and she let go of the gate and hopped on one leg, rubbing her toe. Just then a pony mare pushed past her, through the gateway and into the lane. Before I could stop the escaping mare she trotted up the lane towards the forest.

She was a beautiful mare – golden in colour, with a coat like satin and a flaxen mane and tail.

'A palomino!' gasped Babs, still hopping

but managing to shut the gate. 'She must be valuable.' She was unknotting Patch's reins. 'Come on, Jackie! We've got to stop her.'

I was already on Misty's back. She did not want to leave the other ponies, but I legged her to a canter. With Babs and Patch beside us, we pounded along the sandy path after the truant palomino.

When the palomino heard Misty's and Patch's hooves behind her, she broke into a gallop and there we were, going faster and faster, with the mare being driven still farther away from her home field.

I slowed Misty to a walk. 'This is no use,' I said over my shoulder to Babs. 'We'll pull up for a moment, and give the palomino a chance to calm down. If we go on chasing her she'll bolt for miles, and then she'll be really lost.'

We reined up, and Misty and Patch stood with heaving sides, getting back their breath.

A few moments later Babs glanced at me excitedly. We could hear slower hoof-beats, and they were coming towards us. The palomino must have decided to go back to join her pony companions.

I slid off Misty and stood by her head, ready to catch the golden mare as she passed.

'We've got to keep calm,' I whispered to Babs. 'We must move quietly because we don't want to scare her again.'

We waited, our gaze on the bend. Then, above a clump of gorse, we saw a human head and, next moment, a man came into view. He was leading the runaway palomino. He was a tall, broad-shouldered man in jacket and breeches and Newmarket boots and he had a bushy, 'handlebar' moustache.

'Hullo!' he said, as he caught sight of us. 'So you were trying to catch my pony for me. It was good of you to take the trouble. Goodness knows how she managed to get out.'

'She sidled past us when we opened the gate for Misty,' I confessed, and told him what had happened.

He blinked. 'Did she now?'

'We're very sorry,' I said.

He looked from Babs to me, and he was so tall that we felt quite small. I watched his moustache to see if it was bristling with anger! Was he going to be cross with us?

'I can see you're sorry,' he said after a moment. 'So I'll say no more about it. I just want you to promise not to let your ponies stray round this way again.'

'Oh, we do promise,' I told him.

'Fair enough!' He turned to stroke the neck of the palomino, then smiled at us. 'How much do you think this pony is worth?'

'I don't know,' said Babs.

'A lot,' the man declared. Americans are prepared to pay a huge amount for a thoroughbred Welsh palomino brood mare.'

We listened, fascinated, as the man told us about his Pony Farm. He really seemed to like talking to us about his ponies, and he became quite friendly.

We learnt that his name was Gerard – Wing-Commander Gerard, that he had retired from the RAF, and started this Pony Farm with his wife. He had begun five years ago with only a few good mares. He had sold their foals in America and bought more mares, kept the best of the foals this time, and now had more than sixty ponies.

Then he turned his attention to Misty. He could see that she was a Welsh pony, and he was very interested when I told him how I had won her in an essay competition and that Babs and I were helping out at Pinewoods Pony Trekking Centre.

Suddenly I glanced at my watch and realized that it was twenty-five to seven. The trekkers should have sat down to their high tea thirty-five minutes ago – and we had not even got the groceries!

We hurriedly said goodbye to the Wing-Commander, mounted our ponies, and set off at a canter along a sandy track towards the village.

We had other delays. The track led down a rough hillside where we had to dismount and lead the ponies. There were some stepping stones across a stream but, of course, Misty and Patch could not cross on the stones and had to ford the stream lower down. We came to a cattle-grid leading on to the road, but the gate beside the grid had been padlocked by the Forestry Commission, and so we had to ride along the fields until we came to a gate that we could open.

The church clock was striking seven when we at last reined up by Mr Owen's, the grocer's. Outside the shop was Mr Owen himself, looking flustered as he bent over the bonnet of his van, grease streaks on his white shopcoat.

'Come for the groceries, have you?' he sing-songed. 'Too late, you are! Mr Collins picked them up half an hour ago – had to come over specially. Angry he was, what with you lost girls as well as his lost groceries.'

'Gosh!' I gasped. 'More trouble.'

'But we're not to blame for the groceries not being delivered in the first place,' protested Babs.

'And I am not to blame either,' reasoned Mr Owen. 'Not my fault, is it, that my van breaks down, and the telephone goes dead all in one afternoon. Now back with you to Pinewoods and be prepared for fireworks from Mr Collins and the others. Angry they will be with you and I don't blame them. Waiting for their tea they have been – hungry and nothing to eat. There'll be trouble for the two of you, for sure.'

CHAPTER ELEVEN

A FAMOUS SHOW-JUMPER

'So there you are!' Susan exclaimed as we walked into the dining room at Pinewoods half an hour later. The trekkers barely looked up from their belated meal. John just glared at us, and even Tessa and Susan did not seem particularly pleased.

I groaned. We were in disgrace with everybody.

'Your tea's keeping warm in the bottom oven,' Tessa told us, stonily.

'Not that you deserve any,' added John. 'Why didn't you go straight to the grocer's instead of dawdling round the Pony Farm?'

Babs and I looked at each other. How did John know where we had been?

'We thought it was a short cut,' I explained.

'Oh, Jackie, it was too bad of you!' Susan sounded weary. 'Tessa was waiting to get the tea; everyone came in hungry, and poor John had to ride over to get the groceries that you two were supposed to have fetched.'

'And if that wasn't enough,' said John, 'the telephone's been out of action all day. Then the first time it rings it's Wing-Commander Gerard from the Pony Farm speaking. And we hear how you let out his valuable palomino mare.'

'I'm sure he didn't blame us,' Babs protested. 'He couldn't have been nicer when we explained how it happened.'

'In fact,' I added, 'he seemed to take a great liking to us.'

'Apparently,' John said dryly. 'He and his wife have invited you both to tea tomorrow. Oh yes, you were being a great social success while we were all starving here.'

'Anyway,' Susan added, 'you aren't the only ones who've made a hit. We've all been invited by Mr Rorkins to go to the White Heather tomorrow afternoon and evening. He wants to have a big turn-out to meet Pam Whyte.'

'Weren't we invited, too?' Babs asked, hurt.

'Yes,' said John. 'You were particularly mentioned.' He got up from the table, walked to the window and then turned to face us.

'But, mercifully for us, you've got a previous engagement, haven't you? You're going to tea at the Pony Farm.'

John's news came as a shattering blow to Babs and me. Naturally, at any other time we would have been delighted to be going to tea at the Pony Farm, but now we could not bear to have to miss seeing Pam Whyte at the White Heather.

We felt defeated, or at least, I did. Babs, too, seemed thoughtful, and when we all met in the paddock for a camp-fire sing-song, I noticed that she was not singing with her usual gusto. After three songs she got up and touched my arm.

'I'll be back in a minute, Jackie,' she whispered. 'There's something I want to do.'

As soon as she had gone I felt misgivings. I was about to go in search of her, when she came back smiling and announced to everyone:

'Jackie and I will be able to come with you to the White Heather tomorrow after all.'

'You'll what!' John echoed, horrified.

'Yes,' confirmed Babs. 'I've just telephoned Mrs Gerard and explained. She was perfectly sweet about it. She said that we could go to tea at the Pony Farm the next day and that she was very glad I'd been sensible enough to telephone her, because she'd have hated us to miss the chance of meeting Pam Whyte.'

John stared from Babs to me, and then back again.

'I'm speechless,' he said after a moment. 'You two really are the end!'

Susan gave a weary smile. 'Very well,' she sighed, 'you may come with us. But I do think you ought to have confided in us, Babs, before altering the arrangements.'

'Don't worry, Susan,' Babs said, her blithe self again. 'We'll behave ourselves at the White Heather. We'll be a credit to you all.'

'What a super place!' Babs enthused next day.

Yes, the White Heather was a wonderful trekking centre. The house was an old Welsh mansion with pitch-pine floors and a galleried staircase. There was a big-country-house atmosphere, with antique furniture, a large lounge with chintzy armchairs for everybody, flower arrangements everywhere and a conservatory with red, pink and purple climbing geraniums reaching to the roof. Outside was a simply marvellous garden with velvety lawns and colourful borders. And of course the stables, paddocks, tack-room and offices were as wonderfully equipped as you would expect in such a place.

Miss Drew, Ronald Green and Helen and Diane were there and Mr and Mrs Rorkins were kind and charming to everybody. In fact they seemed to be making a special fuss of us all, and particularly of Susan and Tessa and John, as though they were feeling guilty and wanted to make up to them for having taken away three of their trekkers.

We had been at the White Heather only a few minutes when a black sports car came up the drive followed by a horse-box. Pam Whyte got out of the car. She looked even prettier than she did on television and in the photographs we had seen of her in newspapers and magazines. Mr and Mrs Rorkins went across to greet her. Meanwhile another girl was getting out of the front of the horse-box and letting down the ramp.

Babs and I craned forward, thrilled. We were about to see the great Acushla. And there she was. The girl-groom led her down the ramp – a tall blue-roan mare with a black mane and tail, a white star on her forehead and a white stocking on her near hind. She was about sixteen hands, with plenty of bone and wonderful springy hocks. Looking at her it was easy to imagine her clearing the tremendous competition fences, and winning that Olympic medal and all the other trophies she had brought home from Rome and Madrid and South America.

Everyone gaped in excitement.

Now Pam Whyte was leading Mr and Mrs Rorkins across to meet Acushla and her groom. They exchanged greetings and then Wendy, the girl-groom, handed Acushla over to Pam Whyte. Mr Rorkins gave Pam a leg up into the saddle and then, with all of us following, she rode Acushla towards the White Heather jumping paddock where newly-painted obstacles had been set up.

During the first round Acushla faulted at the triple-bars and we all felt sympathetic because it seemed that even great show-jumper's horses had their off moments. Pam Whyte took her round again, and this time the Olympic mare made no mistakes. Post-and-rails, wall, stile, triple-bars, road-closed, in-and-out with three fences – Acushla cleared them all while we clapped and cheered ourselves hoarse.

Then Pam asked for the jumps to be raised

until they looked really formidable. But frightening though they were, Acushla seemed to jump them even better than when they were low. I suppose they were nearer the height that she was accustomed to jump. After two more rounds, Pam Whyte dismounted and led Acushla across to us.

The mare did not mind so many people crowding round and admiring her. She seemed to enjoy the fuss. Babs managed to pat her flank, and I got near enough to stroke her neck.

Acushla turned her head to me and suddenly I seemed to forget that she was the great Olympic mare. I rubbed her between the eyes and stroked her nose and talked to her as if she had been Misty or any other pony.

'There, girl!' I said, with my head close to hers and my hand on her bridle. 'Who's a pet? Who's a fuss-pot?'

Meanwhile Pam Whyte was smiling at Babs and me. I suppose she could see that we were pony-mad.

Babs started chatting with Pam, telling her all about Misty and how I had won her in the *Horseshoes* competition. Pam Whyte was particularly interested because she had written a serial story that was running in *Horseshoes* at the time of the competition, and she said she had always wondered who had won and what kind of a pony the winner had chosen and how the winner and pony had got on together.

'You must sit by me,' she said, as we went indoors to tea. 'And then you can tell me all about it. I'm dying to hear. You've actually got Misty here, have you? Good! I should like to see her later on.'

Pam Whyte was so friendly and easy to talk to and seemed to take a real liking to Misty. She even rode her round the paddock and put her over one of the smaller jumps. It was like all our dreams come true. Yes, we had an absolutely wonderful time with Pam Whyte, and did not realize until later that we were unpopular with everyone else because we had monopolized her.

'You two hogged the whole show,' John told us as we rode back to Pinewoods later that evening. 'It was a shocking display of bad manners, when Pam Whyte was there as Mr and Mrs Rorkins's guest. You didn't give the other trekkers a chance to talk to her.'

We bit back our protests. We had tried to do our best. What was the use? Whatever we did we couldn't do right!

CHAPTER TWELVE

BEWARE! PONY THIEVES!

That night, while Babs and I were helping Susan and Tessa to square up the kitchen, Susan suddenly slumped down in a chair, put her head in her hands – and burst into tears!

Babs and I were shocked. What had happened to upset her so?

'What's wrong, Susan?' I begged. 'Please tell us.'

'Everything!' she sobbed. 'Seeing how marvellous everything is at the White Heather has made me realize that this place is absolutely hopeless by comparison.'

'Yes, that's what I thought, too,' said Tessa. 'No wonder the Trekking Association inspector didn't recommend us.'

'We must have been mad to think that we could start a really good trekking centre on the bit of money we had.' Bleakly Susan looked round the kitchen. 'The White Heather must have cost a mint and we can hardly manage to pay our way from week to week. We've underestimated nearly everything – vet's bills, food, shoeing, and having to hire those other ponies.'

'Are you completely broke?' Babs asked.

'Almost,' said Tessa. 'We shan't be able to carry on to the end of the season.'

'So that means Pinewoods will definitely close down?' I asked unhappily.

Susan nodded. 'It's the end of Pinewoods for certain. Whether we will be able to carry on until the end of our present bookings depends on what the bank manager says.'

'Yes, we'll have to go to Birmingham to see him tomorrow,' Tessa said. 'We can't put it off any longer. We'll have to try to persuade him to lend us some money against the security of the ponies.'

'This is terrible,' said Babs. 'Just terrible! And poor Molly. She'll soon be out of quarantine – and arrive here in time to see everything closed down!'

My eyes misted and I put my hand in my jacket pocket to feel for my handkerchief. I touched something cold and hard and smooth – the pebble that I had picked up from the wishing-well by the Fairy Glen. How could the wish I had made then possibly come true?

I looked out of the kitchen window and saw the moon riding through the clouds above the pine trees. In the silver light I could see pony-shapes. Peacefully dozing was furry-eared Blackie; tubby little Strawberry; white Peppermint with his sweet Arab face; the bigger cobs, Russet and Goldie; John's beautiful Daystar – and all the others.

Later they would have to be sold to repay the debt to the bank. Tessa would have lost all her legacy. Susan and John would feel terrible. And the hopes of all of us would be shattered.

The venture had been started bravely, optimistically. Everyone tried to do their best, but the outcome was ill-starred from the beginning.

'Go to bed, Babs and Jackie.' Susan dried her eyes and tried to be her brisk self again. 'Keep out of John's way. He's very worried; so I expect he'll be even more like a bear with a sore head from now on.'

I wrote to Molly the next night, but I didn't mention about Susan and Tessa being so down-hearted over the future of Pinewoods.

How could I break the bad news? For weeks she had been looking forward to spending her summer holidays at Pinewoods, and perhaps to joining Susan and Tessa in running the place when she was old enough to leave school.

So, instead of telling her that Pinewoods would soon close down, I wrote about our visit to Wing-Commander and Mrs Gerard's Pony Farm:

. . . Trust us to make a dramatic entrance, I wrote to Molly. *We had just dismounted, and we were leading Misty and Patch up the drive when an enormous russety-fawn Alsatian came bounding to meet us.*

I was about to make a fuss of him when he seized the sleeve of my jacket in his teeth, and wouldn't let go!

He didn't snarl, and I wasn't really very scared, but he seemed determined that I shouldn't move. So there I had to stay, with the dog holding my sleeve while Babs tied our ponies to the railings of the drive, and went to tell the Gerards about my plight.

The Wing-Commander came on the scene, and told Rufus to let go. The Alsatian was then very friendly, nuzzling against us, and waving his tail.

The Wing-Commander apologized, and said that Rufus was trained to stop pony-thieves. There had been quite a lot of pony-rustling in the district. So Rufus did a really worthwhile job.

If I had been a real pony-thief, creeping about at night, leading an unsaddled pony, Rufus would have knocked me down, and snarled over me until someone came.

So Rufus must have half-decided that I was friend, not foe, and had held me as gently as he could. His teeth had not even torn my jacket!

Well, we had a lovely time – a scrumptious tea, and we met lots of valuable ponies.

It's nearly half-past ten at night, so I must stop.

I'll be seeing you. It won't be long now. Keep smiling.

Love, Jackie.

Although I was tired I did not go to sleep immediately. I lay there, with my eyes open, thinking about the fate of Pinewoods. How sad that hopes so often soar too high . . . and then have to plunge. Life was full of disappointments for a lot of people.

I sighed, and I must have gone to sleep because I began dreaming vividly. I had a sort of nightmare that pony-thieves were chasing Babs and me, and Misty and Patch through the forest. We kept on calling: 'Rufus! Rufus!', hoping that the Alsatian would somehow come to the rescue. Of course he didn't – and the thieves were getting nearer!

Then, just when I was most frightened, I suddenly woke up!

There I was, sitting up in my bunk, not daring to go to sleep again in case I started dreaming the same horrible dream.

'Are you awake, Jackie?' I heard Babs whisper from her bunk. 'Don't make a noise or shine the torch. Something strange is going on in the field. I heard a gate bang a few minutes ago.' Babs's bunk creaked as she looked out of the window. 'Look, Jackie! Look!'

I gasped as I saw a prowling figure, rope in hand, outlined in the fleeting flash of a light, perhaps a torch.

'A pony-thief!' I exclaimed. 'We've got to do something. But I'm so scared. If only we'd got Rufus with us!'

'I don't think we ought to tackle the thief

on our own,' Babs quavered, scared. 'Let's creep to the house and warn the others.'

We flung macs over our pyjamas, and slipped our feet into sandals. With thumping hearts, we tiptoed down the caravan steps, and across the orchard to the house to give the alarm.

We had gone only a few yards when Babs grabbed my arm, as we both heard the soft fall of pony hooves on grass. We were too late. The thief had got one of the ponies – maybe game little Brownie, or lovely Peppermint – and was leading him away.

At this moment the pony-thief was coming towards us. What could we do? We scrambled on to the narrow flower-bed and flattened ourselves against the wall of the house.

The human footfalls and the sound of the pony's hooves came nearer. They were now on the path. I trembled. Scared though we were we had to do something. We just couldn't let the thief go past us with one of Pinewoods' ponies.

My knees quaked and touched something that might be a large dahlia stake. I wrenched it from the ground, and as the dark figure came nearer I crashed it down on his head.

'Wow!' yelled a voice that we knew only too well. 'What on earth! Who's there?'

The torch clicked on, and, with horror, we saw the owner of the angry voice.

The 'pony-thief' whom I had caught was – John!

CHAPTER THIRTEEN

SENT HOME

'You two!' John shone the torch on Babs and me. 'I might have known!'

I dropped the stake with which I had struck him.

'We're dreadfully sorry, John. Really we are,' I gasped. 'We thought you were a pony-thief.'

'Ye gods!' In the glow of the torch we saw John put a hand to his head. He was wearing flannels and windcheater over his pyjamas. He glared at us. 'I shouldn't be surprised if you've cracked my skull.'

'Here, let me see.' I tried to be consoling, putting out my hand gently to part his hair and inspect the bump. 'Perhaps some butter on it might help.'

'Don't you dare touch it!' John growled, backing away.

Just then lights began to shine from the house.

'What's going on?' called Susan from an upstairs window.

'Molly's precious pen-friends – your would-be helpers – have brained me!' John groaned.

'Good gracious!' came Susan's amazed voice. 'What are you doing out there with that pony anyway, John?'

'I woke up and heard a pony coughing,' John explained in an exasperated tone. 'I thought it might be Brownie, because he's been a bit wheezy since his ducking. So I decided that I'd better bring him into the stable, and give him some cough medicine.'

'If only you hadn't been creeping about,' said Babs, 'we would have known you weren't a pony-thief.'

'Creeping about!' John exploded. 'I was just being quiet; being thoughtful, in fact, trying not to waken everybody.'

Just then Brownie began to cough again.

'Back to bed everybody,' John ordered. 'I've work to do, dosing Brownie.' He turned to Babs and me and added forebodingly: 'I'll talk to you two in the morning.'

Having been awake part of the night, Babs

and I overslept, and it was nearly nine o'clock when I felt someone shaking my shoulder, and heard Susan's voice, saying: 'Wake up, Jackie!'

I sat up, and rubbed my eyes. Instead of her usual jeans and yellow shirt, she was wearing a skirt and jacket. Then I remembered that this was the fateful day when she and Tessa were going to Birmingham to try to persuade the bank manager to let them have enough money to carry on the pony trekking centre until the end of the bookings.

'We're just off,' Susan told us as Babs sat up yawning. 'Try to keep out of John's hair, and do whatever he says. Everything's taken care of, I hope.'

'We'll cope,' Babs promised, still sleepy.

'We've put up the trekkers' lunch-packs,' said Tessa. 'We've cleared away the breakfast, and left a potato salad and cold chicken tea, covered with plates for tonight. You'll only have to make the tea.'

'Don't worry, Susan,' said Babs.

And I added: 'Good luck with the bank manager!'

Babs and I dressed quickly. We hurried to the kitchen and ate some of the left-over toast and butter. We were making ourselves some coffee when we looked through the window and noticed something happening in the field.

All the trekkers were mounted, but John this morning did not seem to be ready to start the trek. Instead he had formed the trekkers and their ponies into a circle and was making them trot round the field while the ponies stepped over poles on the ground. Apparently he was giving them a lesson in horsemanship.

'Why hasn't John taken them trekking?' Babs wondered. 'They can't be waiting for us.'

Next moment we were more mystified than ever because a large horse-box drove into the stable yard. As soon as John saw it, he gestured and spoke to the trekkers as though to say he would be back in a little while. Then he purposefully strode towards the house.

'He's coming in here,' Babs gasped. 'Oh, Jackie! That horse-box! You don't think –?'

Before Babs could say any more, John loomed in the kitchen doorway.

'Now then, Babs and Jackie.' He spoke briskly. 'Pack up your belongings, and get your ponies.'

'So you are sending us away!' Babs said.

John nodded. 'Do you blame me?' he asked, looking uncomfortable. 'Now, no arguments.'

He frowned, as though his head was hurting and I saw that he had a sticking plaster over the lump on his head where I had hit him. 'I've got a splitting headache. Be sensible. Let's part friends.'

'We want to be friends with you,' Babs protested. 'We always have done.'

'I dare say.' John would not weaken. 'But things just haven't worked out, have they? Anyway, you're not going to miss much. We'll be closing down in a few weeks.'

'I know, and that's dreadful.' I gave a gulp. 'We shan't see Molly, and we'd been looking forward so much to meeting her.'

'Well, you'll still be able to write to each other.' John was trying to be consoling, but that didn't seem to help. 'I dare say you'll meet some day. Now come on! I'm saving your pockets because this horse-box isn't going to cost anyone anything. I heard yesterday that the driver was going south empty to pick up some horses. He's taking you as a favour to me.'

Babs looked rebellious.

'Susan and Tessa don't know you're sending us away,' she accused. 'They're going to be awfully cross when they find out.'

'Perhaps –' John wasn't convinced. 'On the

other hand they may be just as relieved as I am. Now hurry up. Jump to it!'

Gloomily we sat in the back of the horse-box with our ponies. Dark clouds had drifted over the sun, and now a thin drizzle was falling, blotting out the view from the ventilator.

'Goodbye, Pinewoods,' I murmured, and got to my feet to steady Misty who was swaying as the horse-box bumped down the rutty lane.

'Good luck, Susan, Tessa, and Molly,' Babs added, and then began to weep. 'Oh, Jackie! Isn't it dreadful? Fancy our holiday ending like this? And all those poor Pinewoods' ponies having to be sold again just when they've got such a happy home.'

I couldn't keep back my own tears now. I put my head against Misty's mane and sobbed. We must both have been crying for about ten minutes, and barely noticed when the horse-box pulled up at some petrol pumps. We heard the driver jump down from his cab, and say to the pump attendant: 'Ten gallons, Glyn. Fill 'er up. We've got a long journey.'

'But we haven't!' Babs suddenly exclaimed, grabbing my arm. 'This is where we get out,

Jackie. Come on. Bang on the door! We're not going to be taken home. We're going to spend the rest of our holidays helping at the White Heather!'

'Yes,' I said. 'Why not? We were sort of invited to go there. Mr Rorkins told Miss Drew that we could.'

I hammered on the door.

'Anything wrong in there?' called the driver.

'We've decided not to go any further,' Babs shouted. 'So please let us out.'

We heard the driver climb back into the cab, and a moment later, the communicating panel slid back, and his surprised face appeared. 'Now what's all this about?' he asked. Then he must have noticed our tear-blurred eyes because he said: 'Goodness! You two girls have been upsetting yourselves. What's wrong?'

He listened while we told him; then scratched his head in thought before saying: 'It does sound rough luck, being sent home in the middle of your holiday. I don't rightly know what to do. You're in my charge, you know. Mr Collins said I was to take you right back, and no nonsense, but if the folks at the White Heather really want you, I don't see why you shouldn't go. I'll tell you what –' he suggested.

'I'll phone Mr Rorkins and hear what he's got to say.'

He climbed out of the cab. A few minutes later he came back, and our hearts lightened as we heard him withdraw the bolts to let down the ramp.

'Everything's O.K.,' he told us with a grin. 'Lead out your ponies. Mr and Mrs Rorkins are expecting you. Go straight there. It's only a couple of miles up that lane.' He pointed across the road to a lane which led over a humped-backed bridge and then turned to run beside the river. 'And the best of British luck to the pair of you!'

CHAPTER FOURTEEN

FOREST FIRE

As Babs and I rode up the drive of the White Heather the hands of the stable clock were pointing to half-past eleven. Mrs Rorkins, all smiles, came to the door to meet us.

'I'm so glad you've come,' she said. 'I know you're going to enjoy yourselves, though I'm afraid it may be a bit dull for you today, because all the others have already gone trekking, and they won't be back until late this afternoon, but there are plenty of odd jobs to be done.'

We smiled, and chatted, and tried to sound light-hearted, but both Babs and I felt dispirited because of the fate of Pinewoods, and the thought of Molly's disappointment.

Mrs Rorkins told us to put Misty and Patch in the paddock nearest the house. Then, after we had unsaddled, she helped us to carry our kit into the house and led us to an attic room with a sloping ceiling, and chintzy curtains and bedspreads.

We said we wanted to start work right away, and Mrs Rorkins said very well; we could groom the four ponies that had not gone trekking. Each pony had one rest day a week, and today was the turn of Cloudy, Damson, Bracken and Star.

After lunch we cleaned some spare bridles and saddles and tidied the tack-room. Just before four o'clock Mrs Rorkins came out and suggested that, if we liked, we should ride out to meet the returning trekkers.

'Mr Rorkins has taken them to the Dragon's Bridge,' she told us. 'They'll be coming back along the mountain road above Lake Heron. You're sure to find them.'

Our ponies climbed to the top of the mountain road that led over Bryn Cledwyn, and we had wonderful views for miles around.

Below, to the right, lay Lake Heron, and in the distance, we could see a line of pony trekkers, winding down a forest track.

'They're not the White Heather trekkers,' said Babs. 'They're the Pinewoods lot.'

'Yes, there's John in front, on Daystar,' I added, wondering what Molly's big brother would say if he knew we hadn't gone home after all but were staying at the White Heather. 'They won't be coming this way, thank goodness. Oh, Babs, I just can't enjoy myself even though the White Heather is such a super place. I keep thinking about the Pinewoods ponies, and poor Molly.'

'I feel the same,' sighed Babs. Then she stood in her stirrups and pointed to another line of trekkers emerging from some oak trees on the shore of the lake, and starting to climb the curving road towards us. 'Here are the White Heather crowd.'

We rode to meet them and as we crossed a narrow ridge we saw Pinewoods below us. The sight of the house amid the pine trees made us feel sad. We knew we would have a good time at the White Heather, but our hearts were still with Pinewoods and always would be. We could see three ponies grazing in the field there. Suddenly they threw up their heads and began to gallop round. Something had upset them.

'Look!' Babs craned forward in her saddle, and pointed. 'Smoke! Oh, Jackie! The forest's on fire!'

Smoke was rising from the belt of trees which encircled Pinewoods, and had begun to drift over the house.

Flames leapt and we could hear the crackle of brushwood, and bracken, as the breeze fanned the blaze. There had been some drizzle that morning, but the forest was still dry after weeks of sunshine.

'The fire will set Pinewoods alight!' I gasped, and dug my heels into Misty's sides. 'Come on, Babs! We've got to do something.'

We had to take the risk of riding our ponies fast down the mountain-side. Perilously they dodged boulders, and sometimes slithered on the loose stones.

Babs and I crouched over our ponies' necks, and kept our reins short, so that we could hold up their heads if they stumbled. By a miracle we reached the valley without mishap.

We galloped neck and neck. Then, when we neared the fire, Misty and Patch jibbed. The smoke and roar of the flames frightened them. So we tied up the ponies at a safe distance and ran to grab the long-handled, red-painted fire shovels that hung from a stand near Pinewoods. Beating wildly, we tried to damp down the ever-creeping line of flame. The smoke stung our eyes, and choked us, but frantically we went on beating.

Above the crackle of the fire we heard the thud of galloping hooves, and a moment later saw John plunging towards the blaze brandishing a shovel.

Through the swirling smoke he caught sight of me and yelled: 'Run to the house, Jackie, and 'phone the fire-brigade!'

He must have been surprised to see us there, but there was no time for him to say anything else.

I had gone only a few yards when I heard Babs suddenly shout: 'Jackie! Come back! Help!'

I turned and saw John sprawled on the ground with the flames leaping in a half-circle round him.

'He must have tripped over a bramble,' Babs exclaimed, in a frenzy of despair. 'He seems to have knocked himself out! Quick!'

We ran into the smoke, and seized John by the arms. He was a dead-weight. Only slowly could we drag him over the bumpy ground. The flames were gaining on us. In a few more moments they would encircle us and we would be trapped.

'Tug!' urged Babs, her voice hoarse with fright. 'Pull harder, Jackie. We'll never get him clear.'

Staggering, choking, our eyes streaming, we made a tremendous effort. Somehow we managed to pull John clear of the flames. Then, a few moments later, voices, shouts and the tramp of people seemed to be all around us amid the smoke.

John must have galloped ahead of the trekkers. Now they had caught up and were all helping. Someone had telephoned the fire-brigade. Everyone armed themselves with shovels, spades and brooms to beat back the flames that threatened Pinewoods.

I shuddered as I saw that the ground where John had lain a moment before was now a red blaze. I was still coughing and gasping for air. My arms and chest ached. My head swam, and I must have looked shaky, because I felt someone put an arm round me, and lead me out of the smoke.

I saw John propped against a rock and being brought round by some of the trekkers. Then more and more people seemed to come on the scene – foresters in Land-Rovers and Mr Rorkins and the White Heather trekkers.

Above the noise of voices, the crackle of flames, the beat of the shovels, and the whinny-ing of frightened ponies, came the whine of the fire-engine siren, and my eyes stung because, in my wretchedness, I felt sure that they were too late to save Pinewoods.

CHAPTER FIFTEEN

PINEWOODS FOR EVER

I need not have despaired.

After fighting the forest fire for more than two hours, the firemen managed to bring it under control and Pinewoods was no longer in danger of being burnt down.

Babs and I watched numbly. Our eyes smarted with the smoke and our throats were parched. We could not escape the acrid smell of damp, smouldering wood. It was a sad sight. The grass was blackened and the edge of the lovely forest was scorched. The water from the fire hoses had turned the ground to mud. Three lines of hoses stretched from the lake to the fire pumps and hundreds of gallons of water must have been used to douse the flames.

'Tea up!' Miss Drew called at last from the kitchen window and steaming jugs were passed to the thirsty fire-fighters. Mr Rorkins and both parties of trekkers were mopping their smudged faces, and relaxing, relieved that the battle against the forest enemy – fire – had this time been fought and won.

'All because of a piece of broken glass catching the sun's rays, or perhaps some walker throwing down a still-burning cigarette end,' said one of the firemen as he drained his mug of tea.

He grinned at Babs and me. 'So you're the two young heroines, are you? I hear you were first on the scene, and then you dragged Mr Collins to safety.'

Just then John came up to us and, to our surprise, shook our hands, and patted our backs.

'Well done!' he told us warmly. 'Lucky for me, and for Pinewoods, that you took matters into your own hands, and refused to go home after all.'

We could hardly believe our ears. John was actually pleased with us!

'I'll have a word with Mr Rorkins,' he added, 'and I'm sure it will be all right with him and his wife if you would like to come back to Pinewoods, and stay here for as long as we keep going. Mind you, that may be only a week or two more.'

'Back to the caravan in the orchard!' said Babs. 'Yippee!'

Our hearts leapt again as we heard two voices from the driveway – Tessa's and Susan's. They must have just got back from Birmingham, probably with the bank manager's permission to carry on for a few weeks longer until the end of the season.

Eagerly we looked towards the doorway, and in walked Susan and Tessa.

We gaped in surprise. Susan and Tessa were not alone. With them was a girl of about our own age. She had curly, auburn hair, blue eyes, and a sprinkling of freckles.

'Molly!' I gasped.

'Jackie!' Molly ran towards us. She seemed just as thrilled to meet us as we were to meet her. 'Babs!'

We hugged each other, all talking at once, trying to make up for the time we had lost while Molly had been in quarantine with chicken-pox.

'You're both just as I'd imagined.' Molly stood back to look at us in turn. 'What fun we're going to have! And thanks for helping to stop the place being burnt down before I'd even got here.'

'We were beginning to think we'd never meet you,' said Babs.

'Me, too.' Molly's eyes sparkled. 'I used to read your letters over and over again, Jackie.'

Just then Mr Rorkins and John, who had been talking together, came over to us.

'Susan! Tessa!' John called across the kitchen. 'Listen to this. Mr Rorkins has had an idea.'

'And I'm sure it's a good one,' Mr Rorkins added, smiling. 'My wife and I have talked it over several times. John, here, has been telling me some of your problems, so I thought I wouldn't wait any longer to tell you what I had in mind.'

Molly, Babs, and I glanced excitedly at each other. Was Pinewoods going to be saved at the eleventh hour?

John was smiling and relaxed. He glanced gratefully at the older man and said: 'Mr Rorkins has suggested a sort of merger.'

'On a strictly business basis, of course,' Mr Rorkins added. 'You see, the White Heather needs to expand. Pony trekking's becoming so popular that we have to refuse bookings. We could only find room for Miss Drew and Helen and Diane because we had last-minute cancellations. Pinewoods could be an overflow annexe for the White Heather. You'd still run the place yourselves, and make a good living out of it, I'm sure.'

'But this is wonderful.' Tessa's eyes danced. Then her excitement faded. 'But what about the Pony Trekking Association? They inspected us and turned us down.'

'I'll let you into a secret,' Mr Rorkins confessed with a smile. 'They turned down the White Heather the first time. You can apply to be inspected again later on and my guess is that, after the White Heather has helped you to make some improvements, you should pass without much trouble.'

And so it was. We were put on the recommended list and Pinewoods was full until the end of the holiday season, with at least half the guests booking up for the following year.

Babs and I and Molly were kept busy with pony-jobs, but we didn't mind.

We loved every minute of life at Pinewoods – grooming and tack-cleaning and, best of all, feeding times when the stables were quiet except for the steady munching of ponies.

We had many more treks over the mountains and through the forests: lakeside picnics, sing-songs round the parlour fire as the nights grew chilly in September.

Of course we had more mishaps and set-backs too, and sometimes John was grumpy, but we didn't take much notice. Older brothers naturally do get cross, I suppose.

We had pony films and lectures at the White Heather, too, and a return visit from Pam Whyte.

Yes, life was wonderful, and, at the end of that unforgettable pony holiday, Babs and I had the best surprise of all – the suggestion from John that we might – if we really tried hard to be sensible and pony-wise – spend other holidays at Pinewoods, helping with the ponies.

Well, we're home now – and it's back to school for Babs and me. For the time being Molly is a pen-friend again a hundred or more miles away. But we can look forward to other holidays in the snug caravan in the orchard with Misty and Patch dozing under the apple trees, and twenty Pinewoods ponies in the next field.

So more happy pony days ahead!